Cornelia and the Great Snake Escape

by Pam Muñoz Ryan

Illustrated by Julia Denos

Scholastic Inc.

New York   Toronto   London   Auckland   Sydney
Mexico City   New Delhi   Hong Kong   Buenos Aires

To Jim, who brought
home a corn snake.
— P. M. R.

For my mischievous Seri.
— J. D.

ISBN-13: 978-0-545-15360-7
ISBN-10: 0-545-15360-3

12 11 10 9 8 7 6 5 4 3 2   10 11 12 13 14 /0

Printed in the U.S.A.   40
First printing, September 2009
Book design by Jennifer Rinaldi Windau

CHAPTER 1
Happy Birthday

Today is Cornelia's birthday.

"Happy birthday," says Dad.

"Happy birthday," says Mom.

"Happy day," says her little

brother, Peter.

"Your gift is a trip to the pet shop,"

says Dad.

3

"You may choose a pet," says Mom.

"Hooray!" says Cornelia.

"Will you get a dog?" asks Peter.

"No," says Cornelia. "Dogs jump."

"Will you get a cat?" asks Peter.

"No. Cats scratch," says Cornelia.

"Will you get a hamster?" asks Peter.

"No," says Cornelia. "Hamsters sleep all day."

"What type of pet do you want?" asks Mom.

Cornelia says, "I want something that is not a dog.

I want something that is not a cat.

I want something that is not a hamster.

And that is that."

They arrive at the pet shop.

"Here are the pet rats," says Dad.

"Goldfish are nice," says Mom.

"A bunny is a good pet," says Peter.

Cornelia does not listen.

She sees what she wants.

It is not a dog.

It is not a cat.

It is not a hamster.

It is not a rat.

It is not a goldfish.

It is not a bunny.

CHAPTER 2
The Perfect Pet

Cornelia points to a cage.

"But that is a snake," says Mom.

"Yes," says Cornelia.

"It is wiggly," says Peter.

"Yes," says Cornelia.

Dad reads the sign on the cage.

"Male corn snake."

Peter says, "He is yellow and orange, and orange and yellow. And he is smiling!"

"Yes," says Cornelia. "He is dazzling, just like me."

Cornelia holds the snake.

"He is cool and smooth," she says.

Mom says, "A snake can be a lot of trouble. Especially if it escapes. A snake is not a good idea at all."

"I think it is a good idea," says Dad. It cannot chew your shoes."

"It will not make puddles on the floor," says Peter.

"It will not track mud into the house," says Cornelia.

Mom sighs. "I guess it will be fine— as long as it stays in its cage."

Cornelia brings the snake home.

"Snakes like a soft floor and a dark place to hide," says Dad.

Cornelia puts a towel inside the cage.

Peter puts an empty cereal box inside the cage.

"Snakes need water and a warm spot where they can nap," says Dad.

Cornelia brings a dish of water.

Dad moves a lamp next to the cage.

"Snakes eat once every two weeks," says Dad.

Cornelia looks at Mom. "See. He is
not too much trouble," she says.
Dad puts the lid on the cage.
"Make sure it is good and tight,"
says Mom.

At night, Cornelia and Peter watch the snake.

"He is nice," says Peter.

"What is his name?"

"His name is Corny," says Cornelia.

"Corny and Cornelia. Cornelia and Corny," says Peter. "That's funny!"

Peter sits up and points.

"Look! He is crawling up, up, up. I hope
he does not get out and get lost."

"The lid is on tight," says Cornelia.

"Good night, Peter."

"Good night, Corny and Cornelia,"
says Peter.

CHAPTER 3
Corny Escapes

The next morning, Corny is not in the cage.

Dad and Cornelia and Peter search for him.

"Snakes can get into very small places," says Dad.

Cornelia looks inside every pocket.

Dad looks behind every book.

Peter opens every drawer.

Mom stands in the doorway
and crosses her arms.

She taps her foot.

She has a frown on her face.

"Here he is," calls Peter. "He is in my sock drawer."

"Corny! You silly snake," says Cornelia.

She puts him back in the cage.

Dad closes the lid.

"This snake is strong," says Dad.

Cornelia puts a book on the lid of the cage.

Peter puts another book on the lid of the cage.

"Make sure that snake does not escape again," says Mom.

"Maybe three books would be better," says Dad.

Cornelia loves Corny.

She sings to him.

She reads him stories.

She shows him to her friends.

Sometimes, she lets Peter hold him.

Every night, she tucks him into his cereal box and says good night.

Then she puts the three books on top of the lid to keep Corny safe inside.

CHAPTER 4
Lost Again!

A few days later, Peter shakes Cornelia awake.

He points to Corny's cage.

"Oh, no!" says Cornelia.

Dad comes into the room.

"What happened?"

"Corny is lost again," says Cornelia.

"Let's find him before Mom does," says Dad.

Peter looks inside the toy basket.

Dad looks beneath the bed.

Cornelia looks in the back of the closet.

"I found him!" she calls. "He is inside my

rain boot."

Cornelia crawls out of
the closet.

She is holding Corny.

He wiggles and squirms.

Mom is standing at the door.

She says, "It is time for a
family meeting."

Cornelia's tummy wiggles
and squirms.

She worries about what
Mom will say.

"Corny cannot live in the house,"
says Mom.

"But we can put more books on top
of the cage," says Cornelia.

"No," says Mom. "Corny must live in the
garage or go back to the pet shop."

"The garage is a good idea," says Dad.

Cornelia does not want Corny to live in the garage.

But at least the garage is not far away. And at least it is not the pet shop.

In a small voice, she says, "Okay."

CHAPTER 5
Corny Goes to the Garage

Dad carries the cage to the garage.

"This is a good spot for Corny,"

he says.

"I think he likes it," says Peter.

"I think he is sad," says Cornelia.

Dad stacks four books on the lid, one on
each corner. "That should keep him safe
and sound."

The next morning, Cornelia, Dad, and Peter check on Corny.

The four books are not enough.

Corny is lost in the big garage.

Dad searches the toolbox.

Cornelia looks in the recycling bin.

Peter lifts clothes from the laundry basket, one by one.

Dad says, "We will keep looking, but there is a chance that we will not find him."

After an hour of searching, Cornelia thinks Dad might be right.

She leans her head against the car window.

"Where are you, Corny?" she whispers.

Cornelia sees something yellow and orange and wiggly on the front seat.

"He is in the car!" she says.

"But the car is locked. How did he get inside?" asks Dad.

"The window is down a teeny bit," says Peter.

Dad runs into the house to find the keys.

Cornelia and Peter jump up and down and wave to Corny.

By the time Dad gets the keys, Corny has
slithered away.

Dad unlocks the car door.

"Where did he go?" he asks.

"I think he went under the seats,"
says Cornelia.

"Hurry!" says Peter.

Mom walks into the garage.

"Why is everyone yelling?" she asks.

"Corny is lost, lost, lost in the car," says Peter.

"Find that snake!" says Mom.

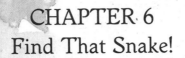

Dad, Peter, and Cornelia take
everything out of the car.

Cornelia takes out a sweatshirt, a pencil
box, and empty cups.

Peter takes out a beach towel, a soccer
ball, and a pair of shoes.

Dad takes out the backseat and turns it
upside down.

"Snakes like tunnels and dark places,"
says Cornelia.

"That is what worries me," says Dad.

They search for Corny in the car all afternoon.

"Look! Corny is going in, in, in," says Peter.

"Grab him!" says Dad.

But it is too late, Corny is gone.

"He might get stuck," says Cornelia.

"He might never come out, out, out," says Peter.

Cornelia begins to cry.

"Don't cry, Cornelia," says Dad.

"I have an idea."

Dad gets a towel and puts it on the front seat.

Dad gets a long cord and plugs a lamp into the end.

He shines the lamp on the towel.

"Remember, snakes like to be warm," says Dad. "It is cold inside the car. Corny might crawl under the warm light."

All evening, Cornelia and Peter watch the spot in the car.

"Maybe you will have to get another pet," says Peter.

"I do not want another pet," says Cornelia.

"I do not want a dog

I do not want a cat.

I do not want a hamster.

I do not want a rat.

I do not want a goldfish.

I do not want a bunny.

I want Corny.

And that is that."

"Me, too," says Peter.

CHAPTER 7
Finally Found

The next morning, Peter and Cornelia run to the garage.

Corny is on the towel under the warm light!

"Hooray!" says Cornelia.

"Corny and Cornelia! Cornelia and Corny!" yells Peter.

Dad comes into the garage.

"My idea worked!" he says.

Everyone is smiling.

Corny is smiling, too.

Mom comes into the garage.

She is not smiling.

"It is time for another family meeting,"

says Mom.

"We have a big problem," says Mom.

"Corny does not stay in his cage."

"He is too strong," says Dad.

"We cannot have a snake that escapes," says Mom.

"Cornelia, what should we do?" asks Dad.

Cornelia holds Corny in her lap.

She pets him.

She does not want to cry, but she cannot help it.

She sniffles and says, "We need to go back to the pet shop."

"That's right," says Dad.

"We need to go back to the pet shop to buy an escape-proof cage," says Dad.

"A new cage is a good idea!" says Cornelia.

"Yes, a new cage is a good idea," says Mom.

"Hooray!" says Peter. "Let's go now."

And they do.